# every color soup

## soup

Jorey Hurley

A Paula Wiseman Book
Simon & Schuster
Books for Young Readers
New York   London   Toronto
Sydney   New Delhi

# We are making Every Color Soup.

# We'll need . . .

purple

yellow

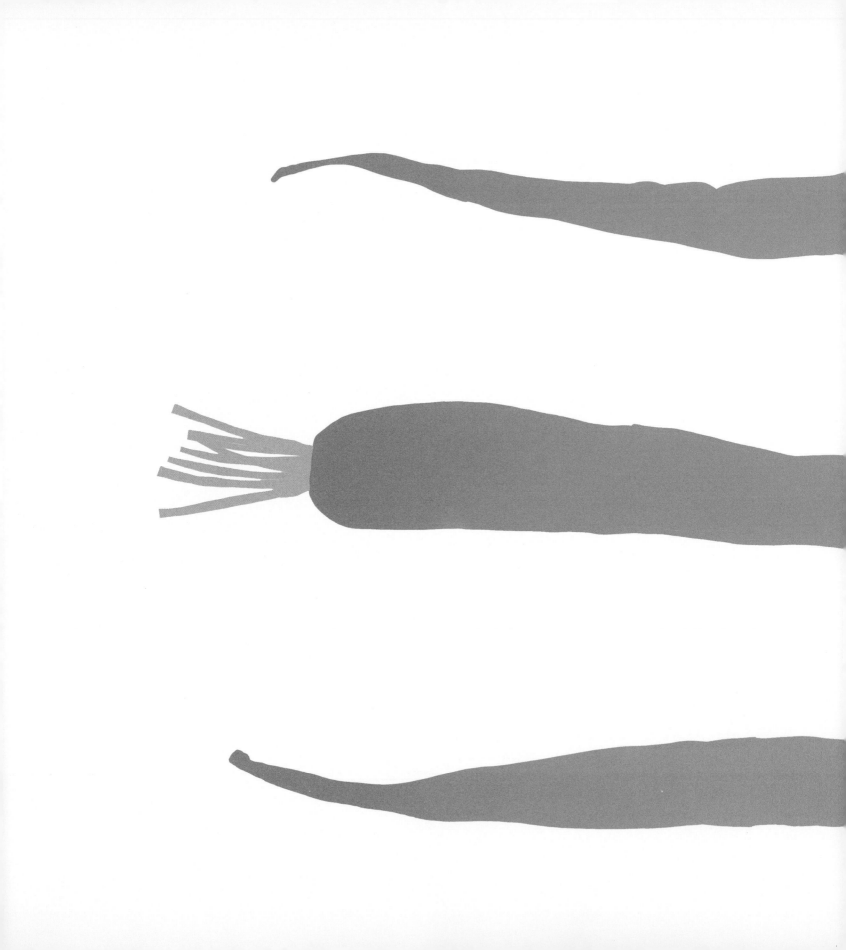

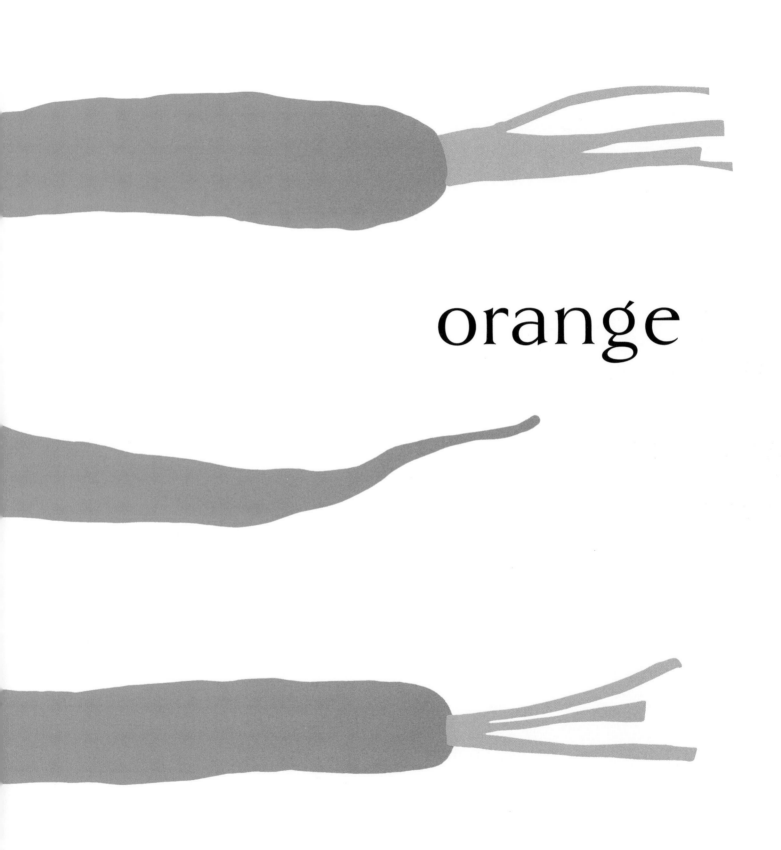

orange

white

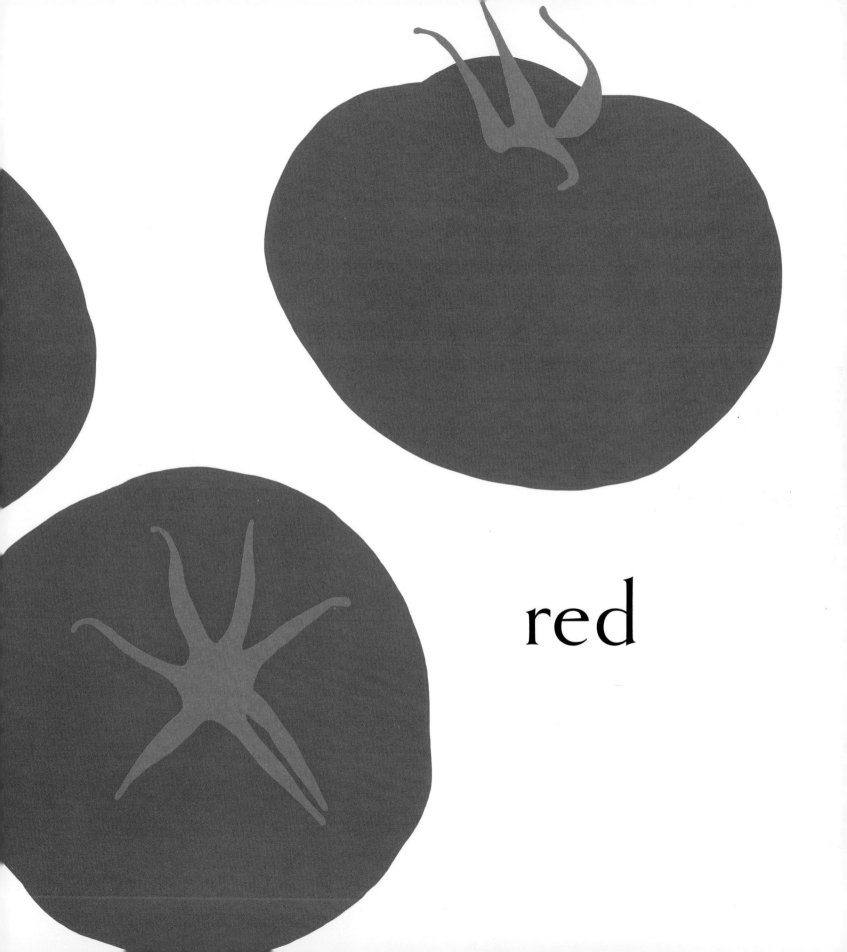

red

green

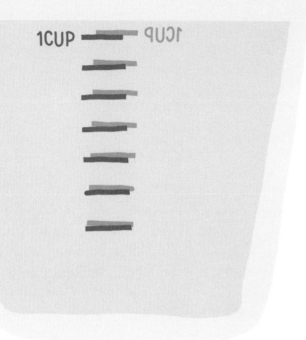

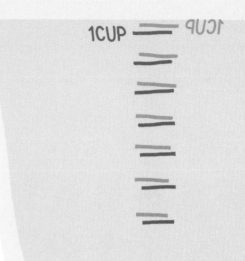

clear

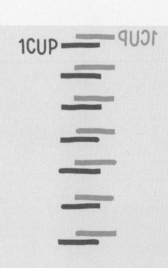

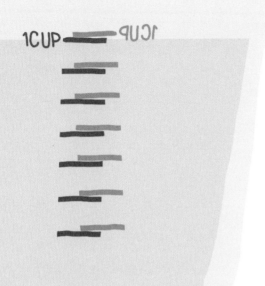

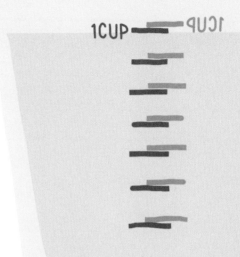

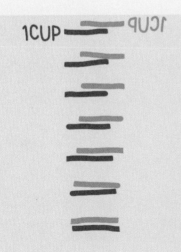

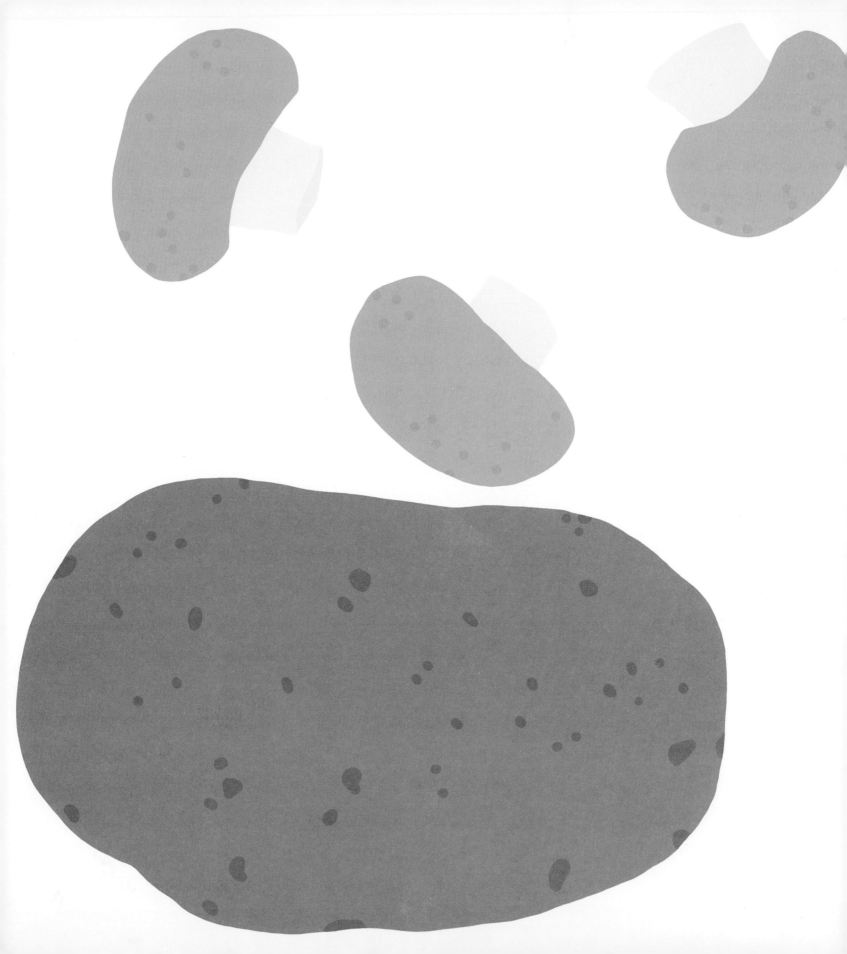

brown

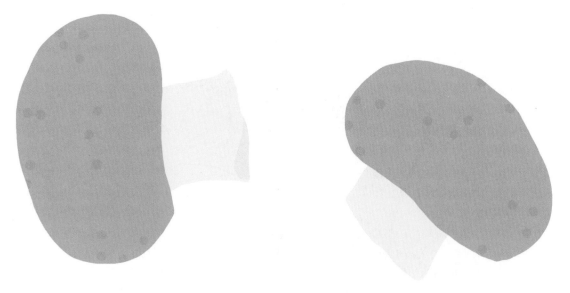

blue

black

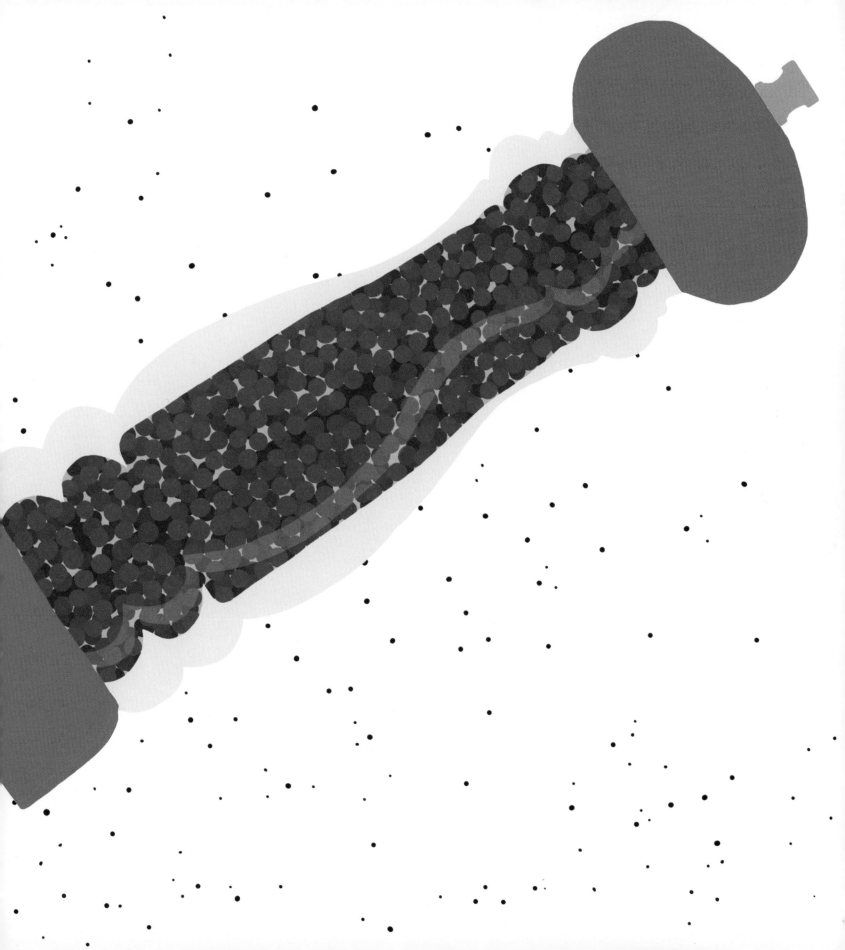

chop

drop

bubble

yum

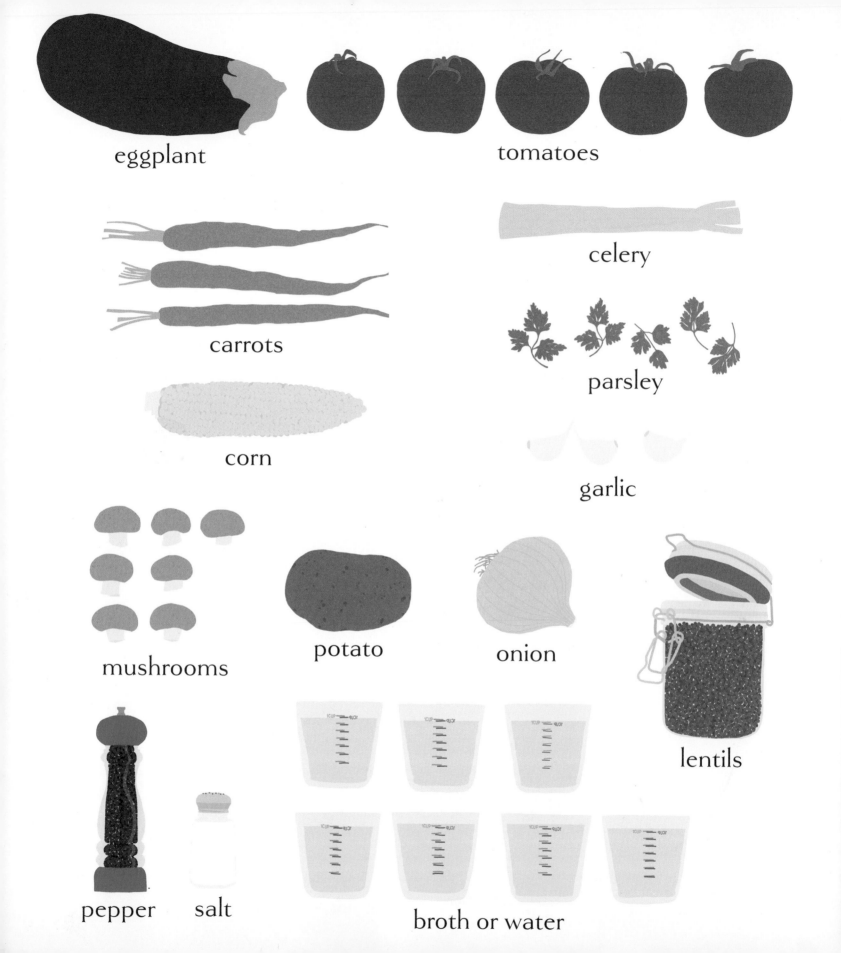

eggplant

tomatoes

carrots

celery

parsley

corn

garlic

mushrooms

potato

onion

lentils

pepper

salt

broth or water

# every color soup

## INGREDIENTS

| | |
|---|---|
| 1 potato | an adult-size handful of lentils du puys |
| 1 half eggplant | 1 tablespoon kosher (coarse) salt |
| 1 yellow onion | 7 cups of broth or water |
| 7 mushrooms | 1 ear of corn (can use ½ box of frozen corn) |
| 1 stalk of celery | |
| 3 medium-size carrots | 3 cloves of garlic |
| | 5 sprigs of parsley |
| 5 tomatoes (can use canned peeled whole tomatoes) | ground black pepper, to taste |

## DIRECTIONS

1. With an adult helper, chop up all the vegetables into about ½-inch pieces and remove the seeds from the tomatoes.

2. Put the harder vegetables (potato, eggplant, onion, mushrooms, celery, carrots, lentils) in the pot. Add salt.

3. Add the broth or water.

4. Cover the pot and bring to a boil on high heat. Lower the heat and simmer, covered, for about 20 minutes. Stir occasionally.

5. Add the softer vegetables (corn, garlic, tomatoes, parsley). Simmer for about 20 more minutes. Stir occasionally.

6. Add black pepper and more salt if desired.

7. Serve hot.

## for nash

SIMON & SCHUSTER BOOKS FOR YOUNG READERS • An imprint of Simon & Schuster Children's Publishing Division • 1230 Avenue of the Americas, New York, New York 10020 • Copyright © 2018 by Jorey Hurley • All rights reserved, including the right of reproduction in whole or in part in any form. • SIMON & SCHUSTER BOOKS FOR YOUNG READERS is a trademark of Simon & Schuster, Inc. • For information about special discounts for bulk purchases, please contact Simon & Schuster Special Sales at 1-866-506-1949 or business@simonandschuster.com. • The Simon & Schuster Speakers Bureau can bring authors to your live event. For more information or to book an event, contact the Simon & Schuster Speakers Bureau at 1-866-248-3049 or visit our website at www.simonspeakers.com. • Book design by Lizzy Bromley • The text for this book was set in Goldenbook. • The illustrations for this book were rendered in Photoshop. • Manufactured in China • 1117 SCP • First Edition • 10 9 8 7 6 5 4 3 2 1 • CIP data for this book is available from the Library of Congress. • ISBN 978-1-4814-6999-9 • ISBN 978-1-4814-7000-1 (eBook)